THE BOY IN THE MIRROR

by

KEITH CHATFIELD

Illustrated by

SUSAN CUTTING

TABB HOUSE

YESTERDAY my brother Humphrey really made me cry.

It all started when he kept walking past the long mirror in our hall. And every time he walked past he pulled a funny face at himself.

"Stop it, Humphrey, you're annoying me," I said, because he was.

And do you know what he said? He said he'd like to stop it but a boy in the mirror kept making faces at him, so he had to make faces back.

"Don't be so silly," I said. I told him the boy in the mirror was him and if he stopped pulling faces the boy in the mirror would stop.

"How can it be me?" said Humphrey. "I'm here and the boy in the mirror is over there. I can't be here and there at the same time."

"You're being silly on purpose," I said and I told Mummy that Humphrey was being silly on purpose and Mummy told Humphrey not to be silly on purpose and not to be silly at all.

Well, Humphrey didn't take any notice. He started walking up to the mirror and then backwards away from it. And he kept looking at himself all the time, which I think is very rude.

Once when he was walking backwards he tripped over Sybil. Sybil's our cat. And she had just found a nice warm spot in the sun which shines through our front door. Humphrey stepped right on her paw and Sybil screeched. And instead of saying "Sorry Sybil," he picked her up and pushed her right up to the mirror. Then he made a horrible face at her in the mirror.

I told Mummy he was being cruel to Sybil and Humphrey said it wasn't him, it was the boy in the mirror.

Mummy said if she had any more trouble she would smack the boy in the mirror and if it hurt Humphrey at the same time well . . . that was just too bad.

Well, I thought all this silly mirror nonsense was over and I was just tucking Cynthia, she's my best doll, into her pram, when Humphrey said he was taller than me now and did I know that?

That really made me cross. Everyone knows I'm miles taller than Humphrey.

"You are not," I said.

"Am," said Humphrey.

"Not," I said.

Well, he kept saying "Am" and I kept saying "Not" until Mummy came out into the hall again to find out what all the fuss was about and I told her.

"Humphrey," said Mummy, "if you say things that are not true you are telling lies and I will not have a son of mine telling lies."

"I can prove I'm taller than Elizabeth," Humphrey kept saying.

"Now you really are being silly," said Mummy.

Then do you know what Humphrey did? He stood in front of the mirror and said

"Magic mirror on the wall,
Who is the tallest one of all?"

The he pointed at himself in the mirror and said in a silly deep voice: "You are, Humphrey."

"He's not, he's not," I shouted. I was trying very hard not to cry.

"Don't take any notice of him," said Mummy.

Mummy always gives very good advice but it's not always easy to follow her advice, however good it may be.

Humphrey made me stand a long way from the mirror, at the end of the hall, and look at myself in the mirror. Then he went right up close to the mirror.

"Look in the mirror, look," he shouted. "I'm much taller than you." It was horrible. I don't know why, but in the mirror he really did look much taller than me.

"You're cheating," I shouted and started to cry.

I thought Mummy would get very cross with him for making me cry but instead of getting cross she picked Humphrey up and sat him on the bottom stair. Then she sat down next to him and put me on her lap.

"Now listen, Humphrey," she said. "I thought you said a moment ago that the little boy in the mirror, who was making faces, wasn't you."

"It wasn't, it wasn't," said Humphrey.

"And I thought you said the little boy in the mirror who tried to frighten Sybil wasn't you," said Mummy.

"It wasn't, it wasn't," said Humphrey.

"In that case the little boy in the mirror who says he's taller than Elizabeth isn't you," said Mummy.

"It is me, it is me," said Humphrey.

"Well you can't have it both ways, Humphrey. And anyway he only appears to be taller because you were standing closer to the mirror than Elizabeth. Everything seems bigger the closer it is to a mirror and smaller the further away it goes."

Then she led me towards the mirror and do you know, I grew bigger and bigger in the mirror as I came nearer.

"There you are Humphrey," I laughed, "I'm much taller than you."

But do you know what Humphrey did? He went up to the mirror and he pulled it away from the wall and looked behind it.

"Now what are you up to?" cried Mummy.

"I'm looking for the boy and girl who look just like Elizabeth and me," said Humphrey. "They're hiding here somewhere."

Daddy came home from work just as Humphrey pulled the mirror too far off the wall. It fell down with an enormous crash and Daddy was furious and Mummy had had enough for one day. I know that because she said so.

"That's seven years bad luck you'll have now, my lad," said Daddy crossly.

Daddy explained that whenever you break a mirror you always get seven years' bad luck and Humphrey's bad luck started straight away because Mummy whisked him straight up to bed. And it was only half past five.

Humphrey didn't seem to mind at all. He said his brain was tired because he didn't understand why mirrors made things look smaller or bigger.

Daddy said he'd tell him when he was a bit older. Honestly, my brother.

Daddy says the mirror does things like that because of something called perspective. That's another word I've learnt.

First Published in 1986
Tabb House, 11 Church Street, Padstow, Cornwall PL28 8BG

© Keith Chatfield 1986
ISBN 0 907018 51 3

In the HUMPHREY *Series:*

My Brother Humphrey ISBN 0 907018 30 0
Daddy's Good Ideas   0 907018 47 5
It's All Humphrey's Fault   0 907018 48 3
Granny Teacosy   0 907018 49 1
Humphrey The Birdman   0 907018 50 5
The Boy in the Mirror   0 907018 51 3

Printed by Quill Printing Services Ltd., Padstow, Cornwall PL28 8AT